I0529886

Pedro Menendez
The Adelantado of Florida

By

L. L. Eadie

Copyright © 2020 by L.L. Eadie

All rights reserved. No part of this publication may be reproduced, stored in a retrieval system or transmitted in any form or by any means electronic, mechanical, photocopying, recording, or otherwise, without prior written permission of the author.

Originally in 2005 under the Pen Name: Effie Mae Shearin

Publisher: Dolly Dimple Ink

508 NW Scenic Lake Drive

Lake City, Florida 32055

386-292-4423

ISBN-13: 978-1-7347371-0-3

Library Control No:

Acknowledgements

I am especially grateful for my family for all their support and encouragement. I would also like to thank the staff at St. Augustine Historical Society's Research Library for their assistance. Leslie Wilson and Charles Tingley, librarian.

Table of Contents

Part I- The Crossing

Chapter I- The Storm

"All hands on deck!"

Under normal conditions, the ocean would be the color of a cloudless sky, but now it was without color, along with the sky above. The sea and sky were as gray as smoke. It was hard to tell where one began and the other ended.

Squinting through the torrents of rain and violent wind I could just make out the white caps of the tall waves rising above the ship's railings and crashing upon its decks. The large galleon, San Pelayo, and its fleet of ten ships were being tossed like rafts in the rapids during this unexpected storm. I clung to one of the tall masts and watched my captain, Pedro Menendez, on the poop deck shout orders to the sailors.

"Man your stations! Bring down the sails!" exclaimed Captain Menendez. "Batten down the hatches!"

It was hard to hear his orders over the roar of the wind and the crashing ocean. And, I was having a difficult time making out his face through the stinging sheets of rain. Anything on deck that wasn't tied down was doomed to the sea. That included both men and boys.

If I had not witnessed it with my own eyes I wouldn't have believed it, but the bow of our ship literally dipped under the water and came back up dripping and creaking with saltwater rushing through its decks. And, it happened many more times than once.

I was a child of twelve years of age at the time – a cabin boy on board this voyage – my maiden trip. I had fancied going to sea for as long as I could remember. I, like my captain, was from the north of Spain. I knew of him long before this voyage. And like him, I had become an orphan and had run away from my foster family.

Pedro Menendez had lost his father and was sent to live with relatives, whom he did not favor either. He took off, too. Pedro Menendez grew up at sea. He had become a sailor at a young age and later fought the pirates of the Mediterranean for many years. I grew up hearing the stories. Captain Pedro Menendez was my hero.

This was not Captain Menendez's maiden voyage to New Spain, where riches such as gold and silver could be found, however, this was his first trip to Florida. He was now Florida's Adelantado, or honorable governor, appointed by the king of Spain, King Philip II, and was bringing two thousand men, women, and children to live there.

"Throw the women overboard!" shouted one of the sailors named Gonzalez as he tried to unlock one of the hatches during the squall. The frightened women and children were down below, where I'm certain, they were being tossed to and fro like rag dolls in their cramped conditions. Sleep was impossible. Even for the rats on board as well, that feasted on our food bringing diseases and death to many.

"NO!" shouted Menendez.

"They are bad luck!" yelled Alonzo, another sailor. "It is because of them that we have run into this violent storm!" He and Gonzalez were not the only sailors with fear on their faces. However, the others were afraid to speak up. Punishments at sea were severe. For disrespecting an officer one could be keel-hauled – dragged by a rope around the underneath of the ship or flogged with a cat o' nine tails tied to the end of a rope. Either one could cause death. And, the entire crew was made to watch as a warning to them.

"Don't be stupid!" said Captain Menendez. "Do your job! And, pray to God."

My body trembled as the sea biscuits in my stomach made a lurching effort to expose themselves on the deck before me. However, my main concern was not falling into the dark waters that lapped over the railings, as if trying to seize my bare feet and drag me overboard. So, I clung to the mast and prayed. Beseeched a God I was certain had finally heard my prayers when I was chosen to be a cabin boy on board this galleon. The ship's priest prayed along with us.

"WATCH OUT!" warned Menendez, as he pointed to the mast that I hugged. There was a cracking noise above me and when I looked up I saw what the strength of the wind had done. The mast I hugged was plunging!

"Up here, boy!" ordered Menendez.

Without a second thought, I rushed up to the stern gallery deck, where my captain stood at the helm. As I held onto the marlinspikes with both my arms and legs, like a baby clinging to its mother, I couldn't keep my eyes off of my hero. I wondered if he was thinking about his son, who had been lost at sea during a storm like this one. No one had heard from him in two years. Did my captain believe he, too, would join him on the bottom of the ocean? Captain Menendez might be bringing settlers to Florida, but he was also coming with hope in his heart to search for his shipwrecked son, Juan.

Chapter II - The Stowaway

Finally, there was silence – no crashing waves, howling wind or suffering sobs from not only the crew but our passengers' onboard. The brutal storm had blown itself out. I was in want of dry clothes, food, and water. All I could taste was the ocean salt in my mouth, and it dried it out and parched my lips. The blue sky and hot sun though was a welcome sight to all on board, including the women and children who were now coming up from down below.

"What is your name, boy?" asked Menendez as he peered down at me where I still sat by the carved wooden railing.

"Rocco," I answered and then I added, "Thank you, Captain Menendez, for saving my life."

"Don't thank me, Rocco, thank God. Your prayers were answered."

"Yes sir," I said as I stood up straight, brushed myself off and rushed from where I had sat. There was much work to be done to repair the ship.

"Where are you going?" asked Menendez with a quizzical grin on his face.

"I am learning the ropes. I will help the men with the rigging. One day I will be a captain of a galleon, too! Aye, aye, Captain Menendez!" I said as I descended the steps to the damp deck below.

"Well done, Rocco," said Captain Pedro Menendez nodding.

That day I learned how to climb the rigging. At the top of the new jury-mast, I could see a large sea turtle swimming by our ship and a school of dolphins. However, I could not see all of the fleet, only one ship. We all said a prayer that night for the other ships' safety as the sun set in the direction of our destination – Florida.

However, that was not the only thing that I saw from my bird's eye view. I also saw a stranger – a man that looked like he was hiding among the women and children on deck.

"Hello, Rocco," said a cabin boy named Gomez, as we swabbed the deck together later that night. Cleaning the deck was one of the many chores we performed as cabin boys.

Gomez was twelve years old also, or at least, he thought he was. He wasn't sure exactly when his birthday was. However, he had more experience than me. Gomez had been a cabin boy for two years.

"Hello, Gomez," I said.

I had met Gomez when we first boarded Captain Menendez's flagship, San Pelayo, in Spain. Gomez was my new friend. Most of the sailors and soldiers on board were *not* my friends. They just shouted orders at me and the other cabin boys.

"Did you hear, Rocco, we had a stowaway on board?" asked Gomez.

"No. Who was it?" I asked, remembering now the stranger that I saw.

"The man is called Pedro de Valdes and he was to stay behind and marry Captain Menendez's daughter," said Gomez. "I don't blame him. Marriage can wait."

I laughed and so did my friend, Gomez. However, I wondered if Captain Menendez thought it was funny

Chapter III - A Good Sign

That night, after Gomez and I had served dinner to the ship's crew, we sat upon a cannon on the forecastle deck and ate our dinner of sea biscuits, dried peas, and salted meat. Our meal was of the lowest rank and file. We feasted on no rice, cheese or sweet wine - only their leftovers if lucky.

I turned my attention to the ocean as I bit into a biscuit. The hardtack had turned soft from the dampness of the storm. It was hard to believe looking out at the calm water that this was the same ocean. The waves now gently licked the sides of the ship as we sailed west. The stars were so bright it looked like you could reach up and pluck one right out of the sky.

"Were you faint-hearted during the storm, Rocco?" asked Gomez as he bit into the sea biscuit.

"Yes," I said as I lifted a sea biscuit to my mouth, too. "Were you?"

Gomez nodded. "I thought I was going to die."

"Me, too," I admitted.

"Do you think we are lost, Rocco?" asked Gomez.

"No, Captain Menendez uses an astrolabe. It guides him in the right direction."

"That's shipshape," said Gomez biting into a piece of meat. "Rocco, do you have a family?"

"No." I shook my head. "My mother and father are both dead."

"I never knew my father, and my mother abandoned me," said Gomez. "She was too poor to feed me."

Gomez and I sat in silence with our dismal thoughts for three winks.

To my relief, Gomez changed the subject and proclaimed, "I'm going to become very rich in Florida! I dream of finding gold!"

"I yearn to be a famous sea captain like Pedro Menendez!" I exclaimed.

It felt good to have a friend on board to spout with. I liked Gomez. We had much in common.

That night I was lucky and found a pile of dry ropes to sleep upon. The bright stars were my blanket.

Many starry nights later we arrived at a large island called Puerto Rico.

"Rocco, come look!" exclaimed Gomez as he hung over the ship's railing and pointed down at the emerald-colored water.

"Wow!" I exclaimed. I couldn't believe my eyes. You could see straight to the bottom where colorful fish swam and starfish lay on the white sand next to huge seashells.

Our stay, however, was not long on this beautiful island. Our captain, Pedro Menendez, was in a hurry to get to Florida. We would soon find out why.

Our fleet to Florida had been reduced to four ships. At Puerto Rico, another ship joined us. Menendez took a short cut through the hundreds of islands of the Bahamas. They were barren and made of only coral. All was going well until Menendez's galleon, the San Pelayo, got stuck on a sandbar. The crew became tormented by their fears.

"We should not have come this way! Our captain is crazy!"

exclaimed the disgruntled sailor named Alonzo.

"No ships have ever been this way before!" exclaimed another sailor named Gonzalez. "Menendez is a stupid captain!"

These were the same two men that wanted to throw the women overboard based on their superstitions of the sea. I'm sure they would never set sail on a Friday, or whistle at sea. They were not alone with their false beliefs though.

Of course, their cruel words were not loud enough for their captain to hear, but I overheard what they said. And, I couldn't bear to hear this declamation about my hero. I shouted at them, "You are fools! Menendez is a magnificent captain!"

"What? Who said that?" asked the two angry sailors as they turned to glare at me.

"Come here, boy! I will teach you not to squabble to me!" exclaimed Alonzo.

"Yes! We will hang you by your thumbs from the tallest mast!" added Gonzalez.

Not only was my head shaking, but my entire body began to quake as a backed away from these two sailors. They headed in my direction with their eyes glaring and their hands ready to snatch me up when all of a sudden they tarried.

"It doesn't matter what he said," said Ricardo, an old mariner, as he stepped in front of them and took me by the arm. He led me away from the two bad-tempered sailors.

"What do you know anyhow, boy?" shouted Gonzalez at me.

Then Alonzo yelled, "You are the fool, boy!"

Old Ricardo called back over his shoulder at them, "That's

right. He is only a boy. Leave him be."

"He has much to learn!" said Gonzalez.

"Yes," agreed old Ricardo as he nodded his head while we jaunted away from them.

"Come on, boy." Old Ricardo put his hand on my elbow and led me down into the hold of the ship. We sloshed in water up to my ankles. There were already sailors down here scraping, re-caulking and tarring the weakened hull.

Old Ricardo handed me a bucket. "This should keep you busy and out of trouble for a while. Clean out the animals' stalls, boy."

"Yes, sir," I said reaching for it.

"And, boy, for now on – hold your tongue. That is unless you want it sliced from your mouth and served to you on a sea biscuit for dinner."

"No, sir, I mean, yes, sir, I won't speak another word to them."

Old Ricardo shook his head and mumbled something as he left.

To think, the first time I saw old Ricardo, I was frightened of him. He was missing one eye and many teeth, and those left in his head were rotten. My friend, Ricardo, informed me old Ricardo suffered from scurvy. I thought he was a pirate. I now knew that I could count on old Ricardo to be my friend, too. The sailors were right, though, I did have much to learn – and keeping my mouth shut was just one lesson.

When the tide rolled in we set sail once again. Captain Menendez, had found a channel. It was deep enough for us to sail all the way to Florida.

That night as old Ricardo taught Gomez and me how to tie a Spanish knot in the ropes, a bright comet made its way across the sky in the direction of Florida.

"That is a good sign!" exclaimed old Ricardo pointing to the heavens, and all the sailors on deck agreed with him. Another lesson learned.

Chapter IV- The Timucua Indians

We sailed for seven days through the islands of the Bahamas. Finally, at last, there it was – Florida! Pedro Menendez's flagship, the San Pelayo, led the four ships along its sandy coastline. During the day we sailed and at night we dropped anchor. All we could see were sandy beaches lined with palm trees and palmetto bushes. However, we saw no signs of human life.

"Rocco, when do you think Capitan Menendez is going to go ashore?" asked Gomez, as we cleaned the stern castle cabin of our captain – Pedro Menendez.

"He is looking for the perfect bay. A safe place with a good harbor," I answered, as I studied a map of New Spain on the captain's table.

"Where's Florida?" asked Gomez as he turned from cleaning the woodwork and looked at the map with me. I knew Gomez could not read, so I began looking for Florida myself, to point it out to him.

"It's not on there," answered Pedro Menendez. We had not heard him enter his cabin. We stumbled over each other and into the wall as we moved away from the map table. Once our footing was stable we stood at attention.

"Welcome, Captain Menendez," I said with a voice as strong as I could muster.

"Hello, Captain," said Gomez in a squeaky voice. No doubt he was frightened. "We were just cleaning your cabin, Sir. We didn't bother nothing."

"Good evening, boys," said Captain Menendez as he took

off his coat and hat.

We rushed forward to gather his belongings.

"Why isn't Florida on the map?" I asked as Gomez and I hung up our captain's coat and hat. Waiting on the captain was my favorite part of being a cabin boy. That, and taking special care of his richly furnished cabin.

"Florida actually *is* on the map; however, it looks like an island. Soon we will correct the old maps," said Captain Menendez as he pointed to it. "That is part of my important contract with King Philip II, while I'm in Florida." Using his finger he drew an imaginary line. "I will sail around Florida and map the coastline. And, at the same time make friends with the Indians and teach them about our God." Captain Menendez sat down and I rushed over to take off his boots. It was getting late and the sun had set over Florida.

"I will help you map the coastline of Florida and build many churches for the Indians!" I exclaimed looking up at him from my squatted position on the floor in front of him.

"Me too," added Gomez nodding.

"And with God's help," said Captain Menendez with a faint smile. And then he added, "I'm feeling rather famished."

"I'll go get dinner for you, Sir," said Gomez. He rushed from the cabin almost tripping over his own two feet in his boots that were much too colossal for him. At that moment I was glad I was barefoot. However, I knew the boots were not really Gomez's problem – he was afraid of Captain Menendez. I, however, was not.

At the same moment as Gomez exited the cabin Menendez's clown, Manuel, and one of his musicians, Alfonso, came through the cabin door. They had come to perform for the captain. It was his nightly entertainment.

Manuel was the smallest man I had ever seen. The top of his head barely reached my belt buckle. Old Ricardo had told me that Manuel was a dwarf. However, that was not why Manuel was considered a clown – but rather because he provided side-splitting humor. I stood and watched Manuel dance around the room pretending to fall and turning somersaults. He'd leap to his feet and fall forward throwing his body up in the air and landing on his back. Captain Menendez laughed at his antics.

I, too, found Manuel very entertaining and giggled behind my hand in case I wasn't the one he was performing for. When I turned to put my captain's boots by his bed, I saw a light coming from the shore out of a porthole in his cabin, just as Alfonso started to play another song on his fife and the little clown named Manuel began to sing.

"Wow! Look, Captain! A campfire! There must be Indians on shore!" I exclaimed, forgetting all about my captain's merrymaking.

Captain Menendez rushed to the window – not to strike me for interference but to see for himself. "Magnificent! Tomorrow we shall go ashore."

The next morning Menendez sent twenty soldiers ashore with Pedro de Valdes, their new leader - the stowaway who was to marry Captain Menendez's daughter. There were both soldiers and sailors on board the ships.

Later, Menendez went ashore also. They met with the Indians that called themselves the Timucua. The rest of us had to stay on board, and to my disappointment that included me, too.

"Wow! The Indians are really tall!" exclaimed Gomez as we stood on deck watching.

"They have bow and arrows!" I exclaimed.

"I'm glad we didn't have to go meet them," said Gomez. A tremor shook his body. And, it wasn't from the cold. We were perspiring from the heat and humidity in the air.

"Don't worry boys." said old Ricardo as he stood by our sides. "We have rifles."

Together we watched these strange men who were dressed only in short skirts, from the safety of our ship. Unlike Gomez, I wished I could have been with Pedro de Valdez and my captain on shore. I wasn't afraid. When the soldiers returned to the ship I couldn't wait to hear about the Indians. I hid behind a mast and listened. I knew to hold my tongue.

"The Timucua Indians' house is only a round hut made out of trees and palmetto leaves," said Diego, one of the soldiers. "Good thing for them it's warm in Florida."

"Their food is terrible. They eat frogs and snakes!" exclaimed Rosco, another soldier. He stuck out his tongue and gagged as if he would lose his breakfast.

"And what about their tattoos?" said Diego, and then he chuckled as he shook his head.

"They are tattooed up and down their arms and legs and even on their faces! How stupid they look!" exclaimed Rosco, who was also laughing.

"And did you hear Menendez?" said Diego. "He wants to be their friend!"

"That's crazy!" exclaimed Rosco. "The Timucua Indians are

like animals!"

"But, maybe, if Menendez becomes their friend, they'll show us where all the gold is!" said Diego with excitement in his voice.

Old Ricardo, the sailor, had been listening, too. He said to them, "Menendez is not in Florida to look for gold. He's here to look for the French."

However, I knew the real reason why my captain was in Florida. He was here to search for his only son. There was no way my hero would leave his son behind.

Chapter V - The French

The Timucua Indians had told Pedro Menendez where he could find the French. The French had built a fort along the River May. Menendez told his crew about his plans.

"We have come a long way and soon we will land at St. Augustine, but first we have to find the French. We won't be safe in Florida with the French as our neighbors. They are not our friends. Florida belongs to Spain! The French are not welcome here!" explained Pedro Menendez.

The crew agreed and applauded their captain. I cheered too.

We continued to sail north and the next day we saw a wide river – the River of Dolphins with a good harbor and good beaches. Everyone was very excited when Pedro Menendez announced *that this* was St. Augustine at last! However, we could not land there until we found the French.

The next day was very hot. Gomez and I climbed the rigging and watched the seagulls and pelicans dive into the surf, fishing. I couldn't help but wonder where the birds had gone during the storm. The breeze was strong and our sails were full. We were sailing across the wind. I could see the line with knots in the water trailing behind our ship. We must have been going very fast. I, however, had not been taught yet how to read the speed by measuring the knots.

"Look up ahead, Rocco! I see the tall masts of galleons! It must be the French!" exclaimed Gomez.

Gomez was right. There at the mouth of a large river were four French ships. However, the wind got even stronger and a dark cloud moved in quickly. Lightning struck the water and

17

thunder rumbled. The birds disappeared. Quickly Gomez and I climbed down the rigging. Rain poured from the sky and our ships sailed right passed the River May and the French. When the rain finally stopped, so did the breeze. Our sails stood still and the seas lay down. The French were now no where to be seen.

Wet and cold, Gomez and I gladly stood by the fire box on the bow of the ship's deck cooking dinner.

"Rocco, do you think we are going to have a battle with the French?" asked Gomez as we warmed ourselves by the fire.

"Yes, the French should not be here. Florida belongs to Spain. They are invaders! We will help Captain Menendez and King Philip!" I declared.

"Yes," agreed Gomez. "The French are not welcome in Florida!"

That night as I slept on the bed of ropes again, I felt the breeze return.

"All hands on deck!" shouted Pedro Menendez. He had not slept a wink.

Before I knew it we were back at the River May and there sat the four French galleons. Menendez put his ship, the San Pelayo, very close to two of the French ships.

"Moor the ship!" shouted Pedro Menendez.

Gomez and I ran to the railing. It was hard to see in the dark. However, we were close enough to see dark shadows on their decks and hear them speak too.

"Hello. Where are you from?" asked Pedro Menendez.

"France," answered one of the French sailors from one of

the ships.

"Why are you here?" asked Menendez.

"We brought supplies to Fort Caroline," said the same man.

"Who is your leader?" asked Menendez.

"Jean Ribault. Who are *you*?"

"I am Pedro Menendez. I am the Adelantado of Florida! The King of Spain, Philip II, has ordered me to tell you to leave Florida immediately *or else…*"

"Or else *what?*" asked the French man boldly.

"Or else we will board you in the morning!" declared Pedro Menendez.

"Why not now?" teased the man holding up his fist.

"Weigh anchor and board the enemy!" yelled Pedro Menendez with anger in his voice.

However, the battle was not to be. The French ships weighed their anchors too, but fled!

Part I- Historical Summary

Pedro Menendez's family was from the old kingdom of Austurias (As-too-re-as) in northern Spain. His father, Alonzo Sanchez de Aviles, died when Pedro Menendez was still a child. His mother, Maria Alonso de Arango, remarried and sent Pedro to live with relatives. His mother had twenty children; however, many did not survive to adulthood.

Young Pedro did not get along well with his new family and ran away and was not found for six months. At the age of thirteen or fourteen, he was on board a ship as a ship hand helping to fight the French pirates (corsairs). By the age of fifteen, he was married. He married his first cousin, Ana Maria de Solis Cascos, with the permission of the church. They had one son, Juan, and three daughters. At the age of sixteen, he built and commanded his own small sailboat (patache). Menendez became a privateer and protected Spain's borders from French pirates for twenty years. (A privateer looted legally in the name of their country.)

In 1560 King Philip of Spain rewarded Menendez with the title "Captain General of the Fleet" going to America – "New Spain" (Mexico, Central America, Venezuela, and the Caribbean Islands – Florida was a province of New Spain).

The Spanish ships traded European manufactured goods for items such as gold, silver, emeralds, diamonds, and other valuables including tobacco, exotic woods, and sugar.

Many of Menendez's friends and relatives sailed with him including his son, Juan, who was named general of the fleet of Mexico. Sadly, Juan's fleet of thirteen ships was scattered in a storm off the coast of Florida. Only eight of his ships returned safely to Spain. Juan's flagship was one of the missing ships.

Menendez wanted desperately to return to Florida to search for his son; however, he was imprisoned for twenty months along with his brother in Spain. They were accused of bringing unregistered silver on his ship from New Spain. Menendez believed he was being held falsely, but finally paid a fine to be released.

King Philip II, who also believed in Menendez's innocence, made a contract with Pedro Menendez. Menendez was to chart Florida's coastline, destroy the French fort in Florida, evangelize the Indians, and colonize Florida in the name of his king. And all with his own money!

With this contract, Menendez was given the title of "Adelantado of Florida," a lifetime-hereditary position. "Adelantado" was a title formerly given to the governor of a province. Menendez was the fourth adelantado of Florida. The contract was signed by the king of Spain, Philip II, on March 20, 1565. Menendez was to prepare ships and men for the Florida enterprise at his own cost. He assured Spain he would spend his entire fortune to assure a successful colony. If Menendez broke the contract he would be punished. Menendez was happy about the Florida contract because now he could finally search for his son *and* serve his king.

Pedro Menendez sailed to Florida on his flagship, the San Pelayo, a nine hundred ton galleon. He had named it after a knight who had successfully defeated the Spanish Moors 850 years earlier.

Three weeks into the Atlantic crossing their fleet ran into a storm, possibly a hurricane, only five of the seven ships and eight hundred of the 1,500 people landed with Menendez in St. Augustine, Florida.   Men (soldiers, sailors, and craftsmen) women

00and children were aboard the ships. There were twenty cabin boys and ten pages on board the San Pelayo.

Ship boys or cabin boys were from ages eleven to thirteen. Many of the boys were from poor families who could neither clothe nor feed them. Pages were apprentices and learned the maritime trade along with the ship boys. Both were servants to the officers and worked long hours, often doing the necessary dirty work onboard the ships.

Women were not usually welcome on board many ships. Sailors were very superstitious. The women were to keep out of the sailors' way.

Also on board for Menendez's entertainment, were nine instrumentalists including a dwarf who could sing and dance.

Menendez's battered fleet first landed in San Juan, Puerto Rico the home of Florida's founding family – Ponce de Leon who had claimed Florida for Spain fifty years earlier.

Pedro Menendez's fleet left Puerto Rico and sailed through the Bahamas, a dangerous short cut (many coral reefs) that had *never* been tried before. The San Pelayo got stuck three times. Menendez did this to save time and avoid a possible ambush by the French, who were also on their way to Florida.

Pedro Menendez was trying to beat the Frenchman, Jean Ribault, to Florida. Ribault's destination was Ft. Caroline on the River May – the present-day St. John's River in Jacksonville, Florida. However, Ribault won the race to Florida.

The superstitious sailors were encouraged though when a bright comet was seen racing across the sky towards Florida.

On September 3, 1565, St. Augustine was spotted by Pedro

Menendez along the present-day Matanzas River which the Spanish called the River of Dolphins because of all the dolphins that swam there. Also spotted were the northeastern Florida Indians called the Timucua. They numbered 150,000 in north Florida and were farmers and hunters.

On September 4, 1565, at about two o'clock in the afternoon Pedro Menendez's five ships spied the French at the mouth of the River May (St. Johns), however, a thunderstorm and squally winds pushed their ships northward away from the French holdings in Florida – Ft. Caroline. Ft. Caroline was located near Mayport in Jacksonville, Florida.

A group of three hundred French Protestants (Huguenots) had built the three-sided fort of sod and logs along with their leader, Rene de Laudonniere. The colony of soldiers, tailors, brewers, a doctor, cartographer-artist, an astronomer, and fifty women and children had relied on the Timucua Indians to feed them and finally the Indians had refused. The French settlers were not prepared and were now in dire need of supplies that Ribault was bringing. They had survived on a flock of pigeons.

Pedro Menendez had been ordered by Philip II to "exterminate all Protestants on land, or sea, in forests, or marshes." Menendez had to obey or lose this opportunity to search for his missing son. If he disobeyed he could be imprisoned again.

Part II- The Landing

Chapter I- The Seloy Village

I can't remember a more exciting day in my entire life. The trumpets sounded, the drums beat loudly, the cannons roared, and the Spanish flags waved proudly from both land and sea as Pedro Menendez came ashore at St. Augustine!

Two days earlier most of the soldiers came ashore. I volunteered to go with them. Gomez reluctantly volunteered too. We were greeted by the tall Timucua Indians and Chief Seloy, whom their village was named after. They became our friends and made us feel welcome. We followed them to their village in the woods nearby. They offered us food and drink.

"What is *this?*" asked Gomez as we stared at the shellfish on our clay plate along with fresh fruit.

"They look like seashells," I said as I picked one up to examine it more closely.

An Indian boy came over and sat down by us on the ground. He opened one of the shells and handed it to me. Inside the shell was a slimy oyster. He motioned for me to eat it. I did not want to hurt his feelings, so I did. The oyster was surprisingly good.

"Magnificent! Thank you," I told him.

The Indian boy smiled.

"Are you lying, Rocco?" asked Gomez as he watched me chew up the slimy oyster.

"No, it is good. Try one," I said as I ate another one.

Gomez also liked the oysters and so did most of the soldiers who had come ashore that day. As we ate the Indian women danced for us. Their hair was so long they could sit upon it. Their skirts were made of the grey moss that hung from the trees. It was a strange, but wonderful sight for all of us.

Many of the soldiers began trading things with the Timucua Indians.

The Indian boy sitting next to me handed me one of his necklaces made from tiny bones, seashells, and fish teeth.

"Thank you," I said as I put on his necklace.

I thought I had nothing to trade with him, but he smiled and pointed to my soiled shirt. So, I gave him the shirt off my back. The Timucua Indian boy immediately put on my shirt. I showed him how to button it. It was obvious that he had never seen a button before. His smile grew wide when he buttoned it for himself.

"Thank you," said the Indian boy mimicking me.

The Indian boy next handed Gomez one of his necklaces.

"Thank you," said Gomez.

The Timucua Indian boy pointed to Gomez's worn-out boots. Gomez smiled, took them off, and gave them to him.

"Thank you," said the Indian boy again.

"Oh well, they were too big for me anyway," laughed Gomez as we watched the Indian boy pull on Gomez's boots. The Indian boy's toes stuck out of the two holes in the front of each boot.

"They seem to fit him perfect!" I laughed. Gomez laughed also and so did the Indian boy as he walked around in his new boots and shirt.

"Me, Rocco," I said pointing to myself.

"Me Rocco," said the Indian boy pointing to himself.

"No," I said shaking my head and laughing along with Gomez.

"No," said the Indian boy shaking his head and laughing too.

"Rocco," I tried again.

This time the Timucua Indian boy understood and said, "Rocco," as he pointed this time at me.

"Yes!" I exclaimed.

"Yes!" said the Indian boy with a smile.

"Gomez," said Gomez pointing now to himself.

"Gomez," said the Indian boy as he pointed to Gomez.

"Yes," said Gomez.

"Yes," said the Indian boy.

"What is your name?" I asked pointing at the Timucua Indian boy.

"Lagundu," he said smiling and pointing to himself.

"Lagundu," repeated Gomez and me.

"Yes!" exclaimed Lagundu.

Lagundu became our friend. We taught him many new words that night as we slept in his family's round house. Benches were our beds and animal furs were our blankets. They placed small fires that smoked dry corn cobs under our beds. This smoke helped to keep the bugs away. We needed our sleep, for tomorrow we would build a fort.

Chapter II- The Fort

The Timucua Indians allowed us to use their council house. It was a large hut where the entire village of Seloy could meet. It would now be St Augustine's first fort.

"Dig!" ordered Pedro de Valdes, our commander, the castaway who would marry our captain's daughter.

We dug all day in the soft sand with our bare hands. We had no tools. A low wall with a moat was needed to protect our fort. Some of the Indians helped us including Lagundu.

"Wow! Look at Lagundu's fingernails!" exclaimed Gomez as we dug the moat.

Our new Indian friend, Lagundu, had very long pointed fingernails. So did all the Timucua Indians!

"He will be good help," I joked.

It was a clear sunny day and was very hot. We were all in want of water. I motioned to Lagundu that we were thirsty. He waved for us to follow him.

"Where are you going?" asked Gomez as I followed Lagundu along with other thirsty men.

"To get water, I hope," I said.

We followed the Indian boy named Lagundu to a well.

"Phew! This water stinks!" exclaimed the soldier named Diego.

"It smells just like you!" teased Rosco, a second soldier.

The two soldiers were right. The water smelled and tasted

like rotten eggs! However, we all drank the much-needed water by holding our noses.

That night, just before dark, Lagundu took us to a pond for a swim. He brought his bow and arrows with him but took them off along with his new boots and shirt that he still wore proudly. I saw him earlier that day showing his Timucua friends how to button and unbutton my shirt. They thought my soiled shirt and Gomez's worn-out big boots with the holes in the toes were magnificent!

As Gomez and I cooled off in the pond we suddenly noticed something big floating in the water near where Lagundu was swimming in the middle of the pond. Lagundu was a good swimmer and had been swimming across the pond.

"What is *that?*" I asked Gomez as I scooted quickly back onshore.

"It looks like a big log," answered Gomez following my lead.

"Wow!" I exclaimed. "It's a monster with big teeth!"

"LAGUNDU! WATCH OUT!" we yelled.

Lagundu saw the alligator and began swimming to shore as fast as he could. The ten-foot alligator swam closely behind him!

"Quickly, Gomez, we have to help Lagundu!" I said excitedly.

Gomez and I began throwing rocks at the alligator, but it did not stop him. We had never seen an alligator before. It was scary looking! I suddenly remembered Lagundu's bow and arrows. I had never shot an arrow before either. I aimed and fired the arrow. My aim was perfect! The alligator disappeared under the water with an arrow right between his eyes!

"Thank you very much!" exclaimed the tired Lagundu as he made it to shore unhurt.

It was our second day in St. Augustine. And tomorrow Pedro Menendez would step foot on its sandy beach for the first time!

Chapter III- St. Augustine

It was day three and the fort was ready. We had worked hard all night to finish it. Gomez and I stood along with the soldiers and Indians on the beach watching Pedro Menendez holding the Spanish flag proudly as a small boat rowed by six men brought him to the shores of St. Augustine for the first time. The founding of the city was as exciting as the drums, trumpets, and cannons sounded. Alfonso played his fife while Manuel danced onshore.

When Menendez stepped out of the rowboat onto the sandy white beach we all cheered including the Timucua Indians. I wondered then if the Indians really understood what was happening.

There was a second applause when Pedro Menendez planted the Spanish flag on the beach. Our priest walked forward carrying a large cross. Menendez knelt and kissed it. All the soldiers, men, women, children, and even the Indians came forward and touched it with their lips too.

We celebrated with a dinner party following the ceremony. It was a good day and there was plenty of food for all.

The Timucua Indians were very curious about everything we brought from our clothes to our farm animals, our food, and our tools. I noticed the Indians, including my friend, Lagundu, looking at our supplies as they were being unloaded onto the beach from our ships' cargo holds.

"Look at the Indians! They are so stupid! They don't even know what a shovel is!" laughed Diego.

"Yeah, look at that foolish one! He's trying to throw the shovel like a spear!" laughed Rosco.

I looked too and saw that it was Lagundu. I walked over to my Indian friend and showed him how to use the shovel, by digging in the sand with it.

"Thank you," said Lagundu taking the shovel from me and proudly demonstrating its task for his Indian friends. They each took a turn with the shovel. I couldn't help but think how nice it would have been, to have had *that* shovel when we dug the moat with our bare hands!

Earlier in the day, before the founding ceremony, two French ships were visible from St. Augustine. The French ships boldly came within half a league of Menendez's large flagship, the San Pelayo and the other bog ship, the San Salvadore, before leaving. Neither of our galleons could cross the sandbar into the safe harbor of the River of Dolphins. Pedro Menendez knew his ships were just sitting ducks – the French would return!

"I have decided to send the San Pelayo and the San Salvadore to safety in New Spain," said the wise Pedro Menendez to Pedro de Valdes and his other officers, many of whom were his family and friends from Spain.

The next night Menendez along with soldiers boarded a small ship to finish unloading his galleons. That same night he would say good-bye to the two ships as well.

The San Pelayo was the first to weigh anchor and head south to safety. Not long afterward the San Salvadore left too. It was a late night with a new moon. Pedro Menendez stood on the bow of the small ship and waved good-bye. We headed back to St. Augustine, however, the wind stilled and our sails went slack. This ship had no oars.

"Drop anchor! We will have to moor the ship!" ordered

Pedro Menendez. "We will wait here on the wind to return and the coming tide."

The small ship was overcrowded with goods and soldiers. There was no place to lie down on the hard deck. I was in want of sleep. I sat down and rested my tired back against the mast. The night air was cold and I wrapped my arms across my chest to warm myself. I shook because I still wore no shirt.

At dawn, as the sun rose above the horizon we saw the enemy – the French!

Chapter IV- The Close Call

"SURRENDER!" shouted Jean Ribault, the French leader.

We had no weapons on board. The soldiers had left them ashore because of so little room on the small ship.

I now shook from *fear*.

"Maybe we should try to swim to land!" exclaimed Rosco.

"I can't swim!" said Diego.

"Me either," admitted Rosco.

"*He'd* probably have you two for breakfast before you two could reach land anyway," said old Ricardo pointing to a twenty-foot shark circling our ship in the pretty clear blue water.

"Wow!" exclaimed the men on board as they watched the large shark.

"What are we going to do, Captain?" asked old Ricardo.

"Pray to God," said Pedro Menendez as he watched the four French ships approaching.

Our prayers were answered again and the tide rolled in high and the wind blew from the northeast. Our ship sailed across the sandbar to safety into the River of Dolphins!

"HURRAY!" shouted all the men on board.

"Thank you, God!" I prayed.

"Look at them go!" exclaimed Rosco pointing at the French ships being pushed southwest by the strong breeze.

"A storm is approaching," said old Ricardo as he looked at

the sky and smelled the salt air.

"They will surely be shipwrecked onto the beach!" exclaimed Diego.

"It is a good thing our ships left last night then," I said.

"Yes," said Pedro Menendez as he walked up to old Ricardo and me. "The French ships will be lucky to survive this storm! Now, is the perfect time to attack *their* fort because most of their soldiers are on *those* four ships!"

"How can we? We will surely be lost at sea too!" exclaimed Diego, who had heard Menendez's words.

"Not by sea…by *land!*" said Pedro Menendez.

Chapter V- Fort Caroline

The old mariner, Ricardo, was right – a violent storm was indeed approaching. It would last for several days.

Pedro Menendez was right also – Fort Caroline was not protected.

We left in the pouring rain lead by Pedro de Valdes, two Timucua Indians, a French prisoner, and, of course, Pedro Menendez. We would march three days to the unprotected French fort in Florida – Fort Caroline.

"We will rid Florida of these Frenchmen!" exclaimed Menendez as his soldiers raised their swords, their bucklers, their pikes, and their rifles in loud cheers. I cheered too; however, I had no weapon, that is, until Lagundu appeared with his bow and arrows for me.

"Thank you," I said as the rain soaked me.

Lagundu smiled and also handed me a poncho made from the skins of a deer to cover my bare back.

"Thank you very much!" I said as I gladly put it on. The poncho was magnificent! I felt warm and dry already.

Lagundu smiled and said, "Friends!" as he pointed first to me and then to himself.

"Yes, friends!" I agreed smiling back at him.

I would not forget Lagundu's kindness or my friend, Gomez's. Gomez had given me his two days' rations of sea biscuits.

"Good-bye," I said to my two friends as I ran to catch up

with the marching soldiers and my captain, Pedro Menendez.

The rain continued to pour with no sign of stopping anytime soon. The ground quickly turned to oozy mud as we followed the twenty men through the thick palm trees and palmetto bushes. At times my boots sunk into the ooze up to my ankles. The hard rain that refused to stop turned the creeks into rivers and then into lakes. At first, we waded in the water, then the water rose to our knees, and finally to our waists! Many of the men began to complain.

"Menendez is crazy!" exclaimed Rosco as he held his rifle above his head while crossing a pond.

"Yes, he is stupid!" agreed Diego.

"If this water gets any deeper – I will drown!" exclaimed Rosco.

"It is too cold and wet! We will all be sick!" exclaimed Diego.

"The foolish Menendez trusts a French prisoner and two Indians to show us the way! I am sure we are lost!" said Rosco.

If Menendez heard any of these angry cries, he ignored them all and just said, "Pray to God for victory!"

 I knew to hold my tongue too.

We rested at night; however, the rain did not. On the third day we found high ground *and* Fort Caroline.

It was a surprise attack, just as Pedro Menendez had planned it! He shouted the Spanish war cry, "SANTIAGO!" just before dawn.

Fort Caroline was now St. Matthew and the River May was now the St. Johns!

Menendez, like the rain, would not stop. "We must return to St. Augustine quickly! It is not safe as long as the Frenchman Ribault is still in Florida!"

Chapter VI- Matanzas Inlet

Pedro Menendez received a hero's welcome from the people of Saint Augustine as we returned from the French's River May victorious. Menendez was now their hero too. The trumpets and drums played as did Alfonso on his fife and Manuel the clown danced.

Chief Seloy of the Timucua greeted Menendez with good news – the French had been found. Three of their ships were shipwrecked six leagues away to the south. The French survivors were marching north to Fort Caroline. However, they did not know their fort was now St. Matthew!

"Rocco, are you going with Menendez to find the French?" asked Gomez as I ate my meal. I was starving. My sea biscuits had gotten wet on our trip and had become moldy – little bugs crawled all over them.

"Yes, I am because it is very important to St. Augustine. The French might attack us! We are not safe, Gomez," I explained.

"I agree. I will go too, to save St. Augustine from the French!" exclaimed Gomez.

"Good! We will be leaving tomorrow," I told Gomez. I knew Gomez was probably scared, but he knew how important this was to the survival of St. Augustine, so he volunteered too.

The next morning we left with Pedro Menendez. As we headed south along the white sandy beach we saw our Timucua Indian friend, Lagundu. He and his family were swimming in the blue surf. The once rough ocean was now calm again. A school of dolphin played in the surf also. The sea gulls had returned and a flock of pelicans flew low over our heads.

"Good morning, Gomez and Rocco! Where are you going?" asked Lagundu.

"Good morning, Lagundu," we said as we waved to our friend.

"We are going with our captain to free Florida of the French!" Gomez exclaimed proudly.

"Good-bye, Lagundu," I said as I waved.

"See you later, Lagundu," said Gomez waving too.

"Good-bye Rocco! Good-bye Gomez!" said Lagundu as he waved to us also.

It was not easy to tell by looking at the ocean that there had been a storm, but the evidence was clearly on the beach – plenty of seaweed, driftwood, pretty blue and pink jellyfish, coconuts from far off islands, and pieces of masts, sails, and the boards from the hulls and decks from a ship. The further we walked south the more evidence of a shipwreck we found.

"Wow! Look, a treasure chest!" exclaimed Gomez.

We all ran down the beach towards the big trunk, which sat in the surf. Diego reached it first and opened its lid.

"I saw it first," grumbled Rosco trying to push Diego away.

"Don't be stupid, men! You know we all share the booty," scolded Pedro Menendez.

To the soldiers' dismay, this was a treasure chest full of clothes instead of gold, silver, and money. Most of the disappointed soldiers walked away empty-handed.

"It's all yours, Rosco!" teased Diego.

"Thanks," laughed Rosco as he shoved Diego into the water.

Diego jumped up all wet and shoved Rosco down too. They were no longer laughing. A fight was soon to take place.

"STOP!" shouted Menendez. "We have more important business to take care of! Save your fight for the French!"

Gomez and I, however, found two treasures in the trunk – a white shirt for me and a pair of new boots for Gomez.

That night we slept under the stars on the cool sand and let the sounds of the big waves crashing on the shore lull us to sleep. The enemy slept too across the inlet of water unaware of our presence.

The hot sun woke us that next morning as it shined into our closed eyes. However, the fog lay so thick across the ocean we could not see to the other side of the inlet of water, only fifty fathoms wide. I could hear my captain talking to Pedro de Valdes and his other officers behind a sand dune close by.

"We will give them food and drink," said Pedro Menendez.

"What will we do with them all? There must be two hundred Frenchmen over that inlet of water!" exclaimed one of his officers.

"Yes, you are right. There are only fifty of us. We can not take them back to St. Augustine as prisoners. We can not continue to feed them all! We are already in want of more food ourselves. I have sent for my galleon, the San Pelayo, to return with the rest of the goods for us. We have no choice and neither do the French. If they turn back they will either die from hunger or Indian attacks," explained Menendez.

"Besides, my Captain, they are heretics!" exclaimed Pedro de Valdes.

"No mercy!" exclaimed Pedro Menendez.

And so when the fog had lifted Pedro Menendez showed his colors to the enemy! They surrendered, just as my captain expected.

"Gomez and I stood and watched from a large sand dune surrounded by sea oats as a small rowboat from our supply ship ferried the Frenchmen, ten at a time, across the inlet of blue water. Their hands were tied behind their backs. Once across the inlet, they ate their last meal.

Part II- Historical Summary

The Ceremony of Possession took place on September 8, 1565. Pedro Menendez was officially sworn in as the "Adelantado of Florida." As the adelantado, Menendez had to establish, protect, and command the Florida settlement of St. Augustine.

St. Augustine was settled forty-two years earlier than Jamestown and fifty-five years before the landing of the Pilgrims at Plymouth Rock! The landing was close to the Timucua village of Chief Seloy (Say-low-ee) and the present-day tourist attraction – the Fountain of Youth and the Nombre de Dios Mission. Today a 208' cross marks the spot.

The Timucua Indians greeted the Spanish at St. Augustine. Pedro Menendez wrote a friend and described them, "The ceremonies of these natives, for the greater part, are to worship the sun and moon; they have dead stags and other animals for idols…They are people of many strengths, swift, and great swimmers. They have many wars with each other and no chief among them is recognized as powerful."

Menendez was correct the Timucua were not united and were divided into different warring groups. Their appearance was described as being tall and muscular with ruddy complexions. The males wore their hair in a bun atop their heads while the women wore their long dark hair down to their waists. Both men and women wore intricately designed red and black tattoos all over their bodies. They would scratch holes and streaks into their skin and rub charcoal and berry juice into the wounds. The Timucua wore bracelets made from seashells, bones, fish teeth, freshwater pearls, and feathers. Their earrings were made of fish bladders. The moss that the women wore for skirts was smoked first to rid it of any redbugs. They grew their fingernails and toenails very long and sharpened them to a point. Their nails were considered a weapon.

The Timucuas' homes were round huts that were built by hammering small tree trunks into the ground in the form of a circle. The tops were then tied together. Palm fronds and grapevines were tied to form a roof. The fronds helped to keep it waterproof. An opening was left in the center of the roof to allow for smoke to be released. The huts averaged twenty-five feet in diameter. The coastal Timucua in St. Augustine drank from a sulfur well found at the present-day tourist attraction – The Fountain of Youth. The putrid smell of rotten eggs and taste would dissipate if you allowed the water to sit overnight.

The morning of the Founding Ceremony two French ships from Ft. Caroline appeared off the St. Augustine coastline. However, they did not approach and returned to Ft. Caroline to report what they had seen. The day before, Friday, September 7th, three hundred more people including women and children came ashore. Menendez referred to these mothers, fathers, children, and government officials as the "useless people." Their livestock consisted of horses, sheep, hogs, goats, dogs, cats, and pigeons.

Pedro Menendez believed his flagship, the San Pelayo and another galleon were in danger of being captured by the French. He sent them to Santa Domingo, Hispaniola. Most of the goods were unloaded except for an abundance of food. He would send for them to return when the French were no longer a threat. The ships departed on September 10th. Menendez, however, would never see his flagship, the San Pelayo, again. It would be taken by mutineers on board back to Europe. However, it would be lost off the coast of Denmark.

Jean Ribault, the Frenchman, came to attack Menendez with

twelve ships and 600 men. However, they were blown off course in a storm. Pedro Menendez convinced his officers to march over land and surprise attack Ft. Caroline after the unsuccessful attack by the Frenchman, Ribault, on St. Augustine. Menendez knew the French ships wouldn't return for at least a week, if at all.

Ft. Caroline made the French guilty of breaking the Spanish law: No man could visit Florida (Florida's borders at this time included the northeastern coast up to Chesapeake Bay and southwest to Mexico) without a license from Spain. The French fort presented a threat to New Spain and the Spanish fleets laden with treasures since they traveled the Straits of Florida to the Gulf Stream back to Spain.

When Menendez reached Ft. Caroline there was only one guard on duty during the inclement weather – possibly a hurricane. Approximately 130 – 140 Frenchmen died and one Spaniard. Menendez spared the lives of fifty people – women, children, musicians, and cooks. The women and children were taken to Puerto Rico. Ribault's son and the artist, Jacque Le Moyne escaped on the French ship, the Pearl. (Le Moyne's drawings of the Timucua Indians at the fort vanished. Le Moyne later drew them from memory. These are the only drawings of the Timucua Indians.)

The Spanish renamed Ft. Caroline – St. Matthew (San Mateo). The River May was renamed the St. Johns River as it is presently called today. Menendez left a garrison of troops at St. Matthew before returning to St. Augustine.

Three of the French ships wrecked near Daytona Beach. Ribault's ship was beached near Cape Canaveral. Menendez searched and found them at Matanzas Inlet (September 29th and October 10th), so named for what took place there. "Matanzas" means "massacre" or "place of slaughter."

45

Ribault offered Menendez money to spare his life. Pedro Menendez refused. He later wrote King Philip and said, "I had Jean Ribault and all the rest put to the knife, as was necessary for God's service and yours." King Philip's answer, "As to those he killed, he had done well."

Menendez had a watchtower built at the site. In 1569 a fort was built to look out for British ships. The watchtower is no longer there, however, a later Spanish fort remains.

There were nine wooden forts during a period of one hundred years before the present fort was built. The present St. Augustine fort – Castillo de San Marcos (Fort of Saint Mark A.K.A. Fort Marion) was constructed between October 2, 1672, until August 31, 1695, at a cost of 138,375 pesos or $218,633.00. It was built of local stone made of tiny shells called coquina. Coquina was brought from a nearby island called Anastasia Island. After the building of the fort, many homes were built of coquina in St. Augustine.

Part III- The Coastline

Chapter I- The Indian River

The weather was changing and so was our mission. With Florida now free of the French, Pedro Menendez could now look for his son, Juan, while making friends with the Florida Indians along the way and mapping the coastline.

We traveled by foot while two supply ships followed us.

Suddenly, up ahead we saw a group of Indians called the Ais getting out of a canoe. They were pulling a dead sea turtle up onto the sandy beach. They carried long spears.

"What are they going to do with the sea turtle?" asked Gomez.

"I think they are going to eat it," I said.

"Yuck!" exclaimed Gomez making a face.

I agreed. Sea turtle did not sound very good to me either.

The Ais Indians did not run away as we approached the river where they lived, nor did they try to attack us. We could see their palm-thatched houses nearby. Many more Indians, both women and children appeared along the river banks. This big river emptied into the blue ocean.

Pedro Menendez walked forward and asked the Indians if he could speak to their chief. At first, they didn't seem to comprehend, but when Menendez pointed to himself, they seemed to understand. There was little doubt in their minds that Menendez was our leader.

"Pedro Menendez is a brave man," said Gomez.

"No, he is a stupid man!" laughed Diego, a soldier.

"He is crazy! They may eat him too!" laughed Rosco, another unkind soldier.

I held my tongue and so did Gomez. However, it was hard not to stand up for my captain. Old Ricardo looked at me and smiled. He knew what I was thinking and was glad I had learned my lesson.

The Ais Indian chief approached Menendez as it started to rain. The chief offered us shelter in their palm-thatched houses. To keep the rain out the Ais Indians hung palm-thatched mats that touched the ground around the sides, like curtains.

"Wow! Look at their necklaces," said Diego.

Many of the Indians wore gold and silver treasures.

"That one must be solid gold!" exclaimed Rosco pointing at the necklace around the neck of one of the Indians.

"I am going to trade my helmet for that piece of gold jewelry!" said Diego excitedly.

"Well, I will trade my neck scarf for those gold beads!" exclaimed Rosco.

The Ais Indians happily traded their pretty gold and silver jewelry with the soldiers. I felt sad for the Indians. They did not understand how much more valuable their jewelry was than the soldiers' goods.

An Ais Indian woman offered us food on a palmetto leaf while we sat on benches lined with pillows in one of their houses. I believe the food was fish, but it could have been a sea turtle. Whatever it was – it was *not* good. I swallowed it without chewing it up first. Gomez did the same thing. We did so because we were all in want of food and drink.

The Ais Indian woman next offered us water from a big conch shell. I was sure glad it was not from a smelly well.

Pedro Menendez made friends with the Ais Indian chief. Menendez gave the chief gifts of clothing, an axe, and pretty jewelry. The gift of clothes made the Ais Chief very happy. He put them on and walked around smiling showing all the other Indians. They smiled too and so did we.

Pedro Menendez decided this place along the Indian River would be a good spot for another Spanish fort. He would choose some men to stay behind and build it.

I was glad Gomez and I were not chosen. The Ais Indians seemed nice, but I preferred to be with my captain, Pedro Menendez.

"I don't want to stay here!" complained Diego after being chosen.

"Me either," said Rosco after he was chosen too. Rosco made an angry face, however, he suddenly smiled and added, "But…as long as we are here we might as well get all the Ais Indians' treasures! We will be rich!"

Chapter II- Cuba

We boarded our ship and sailed south through rough winter seas from Florida to a large island named Cuba. Pedro Menendez received good and bad news upon our arrival.

"Good news, Captain Menendez," said old Ricardo after we had moored our ships in the big Cuban port named Havana. Old Ricardo had gone ashore before Menendez and had now returned to the ship to report what he had discovered.

"Tell me," said Menendez as he stood on deck and looked out across the pretty blue water.

"Two of your ships, that were lost, have arrived from Spain," declared old Ricardo, scratching his mangy grey beard.

"Magnificent!" said Pedro Menendez smiling.

"That's not all, captain. They have captured a prize ship with a rich cargo!" exclaimed old Ricardo, now grinning with his few brown teeth showing.

"Wow!" said Menendez. "That is good news!"

"I also have bad news," said old Ricardo, looking down at the deck now.

"What?" asked Pedro Menendez.

"The two ships you sent to find your galleon, the San Pelayo, are here also. But, I am sorry to say that they did not find her. The San Pelayo is lost!"

"I see," said Menendez and then he asked, "Is there any news of my son, Juan?"

"No," said old Ricardo.

However, that was not the last bad news Menendez would receive in Cuba.

Pedro Menendez went ashore to meet Garcia Osorio, the governor of Cuba. While he was gone Gomez and I swabbed the decks. We had not been given permission to go ashore.

"Good day, Governor Osorio. My name is Pedro Menendez. I am the Adelantado of Florida."

"Hello, Pedro Menendez," said Garcia Osorio, the Cuban governor.

"I have come to Cuba for food and supplies for Florida," explained Pedro Menendez.

"I have nothing to give you," said Garcia Osorio.

"I have a letter from Spain – from the king! King Philip orders you to help me! Florida is very important to New Spain!" exclaimed Menendez.

"Cuba is not rich. I have nothing to give you for *your* Florida!" exclaimed Garcia Osorio.

Meanwhile back on the ship…

"Hello, Rocco and Gomez, did you two miss us?" asked

Alonzo, one of the sailors that had searched for the San Pelayo. He and his friend and fellow sailor, Gonzalez, were now back on board Menendez's ship.

I ignored Alonzo and Gonzalez and so did Gomez, who was afraid of the two mean sailors.

However, Manuel, the clown, who was fishing over the side of the ship laughed and teased them by saying, "I didn't miss you two scallywags!"

"We weren't talking to you, little man!" snapped Gonzalez.

"Boys, you missed a spot!" laughed Alonzo as he and Gomez walked across the clean deck in their dirty boots. Suddenly they both slipped and fell just as Menendez came back on board surprising us all.

"GONZALEZ! ALONZO! Get below and clean out the hold! GET BUSY! We have a new ship!" ordered Pedro Menendez.

I could tell my captain was not happy.

Chapter III- The Calusa Indians

The salt lay heavy in the air and filled my nostrils as I opened my tired eyes one morning to a sea of fog after we sailed from Cuba. I could see nothing. The day before we had meandered around a large group of small islands called the Keys as we headed into a new body of water – the Gulf of Mexico. I carefully climbed up into the crow's nest on the foremast of our new big ship, the Santa Catalina. However, all I could see were two pelicans flying inches from the blue water that lazily slapped the sides of our ship. Suddenly, I heard a man's voice coming from out in the fog. I wondered if I was dreaming. No, I heard it again.

"HELLO! HELLO!" shouted the voice in Spanish. (Hola! Hola!)

The sun was hot and was now burning the morning fog off the water. There before my eyes was a man who was dressed like an Indian and riding in an Indian canoe! But, to my surprise, he was speaking Spanish! Could he be Juan – Captain Menendez's lost son?

"CAPTAIN! CAPTAIN! There's a man there in a canoe!" I yelled pointing.

The man was indeed Spanish, but *not* my captain's son. He had lived with the Indians since he was ten years of age. I listened with great interest to his story as he sat with Pedro Menendez on the stern gallery deck.

"What is your name?" asked Menendez.

"Hernando," answered the man.

"Where did you come from?" asked my captain.

54

"I am from the village of the Calusa Indians. I have lived with them for twenty years. I was shipwrecked," explained Hernando.

"Are there any more Spanish captives among the Calusa Indians?" asked Menendez.

"Yes," answered Hernando.

"Are any of the captives named Juan Menendez?" asked my captain hopefully.

"No," answered Hernando shaking his head.

Pedro Menendez's hope faded from his face as he asked his next question, "Will you take us to meet the chief of the Calusa Indians?"

"Yes. I will take you to meet Chief Carlos," said Hernando.

Later in the day…

"Are you scared?" asked Gomez as we followed the castaway – Hernando, Captain Menendez, and two hundred soldiers down a sandy path lined with palmettos and palm trees. There was no moss hanging on any of these trees. The village sat a half a league away.

"No…well…maybe a little," I confessed.

"Can you believe it, Rocco? Hernando has lived here with the Indians since he was ten years old?" asked the amazed Gomez.

"Well then, the Calusa Indians must be nice," I said hopefully.

We entered the Calusa village in parade fashion with our

drummers, fifers, trumpeters, harpist, and Alfonso the fiddler playing loudly along with Manuel the clown singing and dancing. I felt like dancing too. However, that was impossible because Gomez and I were carrying *some* of the gifts for the Calusa chief that Hernando, the castaway, had called Carlos.

The castaway, Hernando, led us into the large house of Chief Carlos. The Calusa chief sat in the center of the palm-thatched house on a stage surrounded by his big family. Some of his family was young and others were very, very old. A Calusa woman sat next to the chief on the stage.

"Wow!" exclaimed Gomez as we entered the Indian house.

It was very large and much bigger than our fort back in St. Augustine that *was* the Timucua's council house.

I don't know how many Calusa men and women there were in the big house, but too many for me to count. The Indian women sat on one side and the men on the other. There were ten windows and outside each window stood fifty young Calusa girls singing pretty songs. However, behind each group of Indian girls at the ten windows also stood Menendez's two hundred soldiers with their rifles ready – just in case of trouble!

"Look, Rocco, Chief Carlos is getting up. Wow, look at the gold jewel on his forehead!" whispered Gomez.

Gomez was right. Chief Carlos wore a gold coin on his fore head and he wore beads strapped to his legs. He greeted Pedro Menendez by placing his hands out in front of him, palms facing up and kneeling. Pedro Menendez kneeled too and offered his hands in the same manner. Chief Carlos placed his open hands on top of Menendez's hands. Now all of Chief Carlos's family members got up and offered their hands in the Calusa greeting too.

"That looks silly. Why don't they just shake hands?" asked Gomez as some Indian men and women now got up to dance for Menendez and Chief Carlos.

"I am sure it is a greeting of respect for important people only," I said softly as we stood behind Pedro Menendez still holding the gifts.

Before we could offer our gifts, Chief Carlos gave our captain a bar of gold from a Spanish shipwreck!

"Come here, Rocco and Gomez," ordered Pedro Menendez who was now seated between Chief Carlos and the Calusa Indian woman.

We rushed forward with the gifts. Menendez took only a pretty suit of clothing with a hat for Chief Carlos from us.

"Thank you," said Chief Carlos as he was directed by Hernando the castaway, who was their interpreter. Chief Carlos put the clothes on immediately.

Pedro Menendez next unfolded a sheet of paper and began to read it. "My name is Pedro Menendez. I am the Adelantado of Florida. I come from Spain. My chief is King Philip of Spain. It is nice to meet you Chief Carlos and your good family," read our captain *in the tongue of the Calusa*.

Chief Carlos, the Indian woman, and his entire family jumped up with fright! Pedro Menendez was alarmed and so were we, for we knew not what words our captain had spoken. Hernando, the castaway, had helped Menendez write the greeting in the Calusa language.

Hernando and Chief Carlos talked and then they smiled and sat down. Chief Carlos's family sat back down smiling too.

Hernando now explained what had happened to Pedro

Menendez, "Chief Carlos thought the paper had a voice,"

Gomez turned to me and giggled saying, "You mean he thought the paper was talking and *not* our captain?"

"Yes," I whispered and then I laughed softly too.

Menendez now continued to read the paper, but this time in Spanish to the Indian woman sitting next to Chief Carlos. "You are a pretty woman. Chief Carlos is a lucky man!"

The woman blushed and Chief Carlos smiled when Hernando, the castaway, interpreted Menendez's words into the tongue of the Calusa Indians. Chief Carlos turned and spoke to the woman and she blushed again. Chief Carlos' family now cheered.

"She isn't pretty," whispered Gomez to me during the applause.

"I agree," I said and then we both laughed softly again.

"Captain Menendez, this is Chief Carlos' sister," explained Hernando with a knowing smile.

"Tell Chief Carlos, Hernando, that I would like to meet his wife. I have gifts for her," explained Pedro Menendez.

As soon as Chief Carlos heard *that* he sent for his wife. When she entered the large house of the Calusa, we were all stunned! Chief Carlos's wife *was* beautiful! Chief Carlos *was* indeed a lucky man! She came over and sat down next to Menendez as he read the paper again, but this time to *her*.

"GO AWAY!" shouted the jealous Chief Carlos to his pretty wife when Menendez had finished reading and Hernando, the castaway, interpreted what Menendez said. His pretty wife got up to leave quickly.

"No! Hernando, please tell Chief Carlos that I have not given his wife her gifts yet," explained Pedro Menendez.

"STAY!" ordered Chief Carlos as his wife sat back down again after Hernando begged the chief to let her stay and receive her gifts.

"Rocco, bring me the dress!" ordered Menendez.

I rushed forward quickly with a beautiful green silk dress. Menendez offered it to the pretty blushing wife of Chief Carlos who put it on immediately.

"Gomez, bring me the mirror!" ordered Menendez.

Gomez rushed up too and handed our captain the other nice gift. Pedro Menendez held up the mirror for Chief Carlos's wife to look in. She smiled and took the mirror from his hands and showed Chief Carlos. Chief Carlos and his wife pulled the mirror back and forth taking turns looking at themselves in it and smiling. She now shared her gift of the mirror with the rest of Chief Carlos's family. It was obvious that none of them had ever seen their reflection in a looking glass before. Gomez and I couldn't help but laugh again as Chief Carlos's family pointed at themselves in the mirror and laughed too.

"Rocco! Gomez! Set the table and bring the food!" ordered Menendez.

Gomez and I set the table with a white tablecloth and napkins. We served sweetmeats, sea biscuits, and pear marmalade. Chief Carlos and the two Calusa Indian women liked the food very much. And Chief Carlos served oysters and fish.

Gomez and I watched the dinner party. Chief Carlos and his pretty wife ate from the same plate while our captain shared a plate with the chief's sister – the not so beautiful one.

Pedro Menendez ordered his musicians to play for Chief Carlos while they ate. Alfonso and the other musicians played while Manuel the clown danced and six men sang. Chief Carlos was so impressed he ordered the girls outside the windows to stop singing.

After the dinner party Chief Carlos promised Menendez his friendship. "I agree to be a friend to your friends and an enemy to your enemies," said Chief Carlos. Then he added a surprise gift, "I give you my sister – for your wife!"

Chapter IV- Antonia

"Wow, Rocco! She's ugly! Why did Pedro Menendez marry Chief Carlos' sister anyway?" asked Gomez as we stood in the crow's nest of the tallest mast. Our sails were now full as our large ship sailed back to Cuba before heading back to St. Augustine.

"Chief Carlos might have gotten mad if our captain had not...and then who knows what might have happened!" I explained to Gomez.

I didn't blame my captain for not wanting to marry this Indian princess. Besides, Pedro Menendez *was* already married. However, last night Chief Carlos would not take no for an answer. He was insulted when Menendez had said "no."

"But she is not a Christian. She worships a devil!" explained Pedro Menendez to the Calusa Indian chief.

"The Calusa Indians will accept your God as our God *and* so will she!" argued Chief Carlos.

Before we left the Calusa Indians the next morning Menendez placed a large cross in their village.

"Antonia, you will need to learn the Christian prayers now," said Menendez to the Indian princess after she was baptized and they were married.

"Yes," agreed Antonia smiling.

"I will teach her," said one of the Christian women captives who was one of Antonia's servants. She had lived with the Calusa Indians for many years, just like Hernando.

"Good! We will be in Cuba soon and there you will live, Antonia," explained the unhappy Menendez before walking back to the helm of the ship. Antonia did not know it then, but my captain would never be Antonia's husband and would later return her to her brother – Chief Carlos.

A few days later we had reached Cuba. We dropped off our passengers – Antonia and her Spanish castaway servant and then we're on our way to St. Augustine. My captain's search for his son was not over yet.

Chapter V- Mutiny

"Rocco, look at the dolphins swimming off the bow of our ship!" said Gomez excitedly pointing and hanging over the Santa Catalina's railing.

The dolphins glistened in the morning's sun as it rose above the horizon. The water glistened too. It was going to be a pretty day.

"That is a good sign," said old Ricardo as he too looked over the railing at the school of dolphins following us.

It was a perfect day for sailing as we sailed before the wind out of the Havana harbor in Cuba. Antonia had waved good-bye to Pedro Menendez as he had stood on the bridge. If he saw her, he pretended not to, for he did not return her wave.

I climbed the rigging up to the crow's nest once we were underway along Florida's coast. I watched the pelicans dive headfirst into the sea. There they rested bobbing on the surface, like a duck on a pond, after they had feasted on a surf fish. From my bird's eye view, I spied a caravel ship.

"CAPTAIN, A SHIP!" I hollered pointing in the direction of the caravel.

Pedro Menendez steered our ship from the helm in the other ship's direction. The caravel did not escape us.

"ROSCO! DIEGO! What are you two doing on board *this* ship? I left you two at the Ais Indian village to build a fort along the Indian River!" exclaimed the surprised Menendez as he boarded the caravel when we had caught up with it.

"They are mutineers!" revealed the captain of the caravel. "They boarded our ship and stole it from us. We were supplying all the Florida forts with food!"

"We were starving to death, captain!" explained Diego.

"He's telling the truth, Captain Menendez. All we had to eat was one bowl of corn a day!" complained Rosco.

You foolish men! Did you even think about the men, women, and children at the other forts? I am *very* disappointed! To the brig with all of you!" exclaimed Menendez with pain in his voice as he now noticed the Ais Indians' treasures on his soldiers. "I pray to God that he will forgive you for your sins!"

Chapter VI- Treason at St. Augustine

We arrived in St. Augustine's River of Dolphins with the mutinied supply ship bringing up the rear. Things looked the same in St. Augustine, but at the same time, things looked very different. There were no cheering crowds this time. And where were the tall tattooed Timucua Indians? I am sure in the minds of all on board, including my captain, Pedro Menendez; the question of what had happened here worried them.

Finally a sign of life! Pedro de Valdes appeared with other soldiers on the beach. Their faces showed signs of sickness *and something else*. Something I could not put my finger on. Was it *shame?*

"Welcome, Adelantado!" greeted Pedro de Valdes with happiness in his weak voice as we departed onshore in small boats.

The women and their children were now visible too. They smiled and waved to us. However, I could see the tears in their tired eyes. They too had suffered.

"Tell me! What has happened here, Valdes?" asked Pedro Menendez.

"I am sorry to report captain, but much sickness, starvation, death, and …" Pedro de Valdes paused and stared at the white sand under his worn-out boots.

"And what else?" asked Pedro Menendez.

Pedro de Valdes now looked up, stood tall, and found his voice once again, "Treason."

"Treason?" asked Menendez almost in a whisper.

I could tell that my captain was worried about the future of his Florida settlements – first mutiny and now treason!

"Yes, captain. Our own men put us in the stocks, but I escaped and freed the other loyal officers," explained Valdes.

"Where are these traitors, Valdes?" demanded Pedro Menendez.

"About one hundred of them have mutinied a supply ship in the harbor. I begged them not to leave us without food for the starving and sick women and children."

"What about the fort – St. Matthew?" asked the sad and disappointed Menendez.

"Treason again, Captain. The disloyal soldiers there finished building a small ship left by the French at Fort Caroline. I have been told that the two groups of traitors plan to sail together to New Spain to find their fame and fortune."

"And what about the Timucua Indians?" asked Menendez.

"They are no longer our friends. Our rifles are useless against their swift arrows…"

My mind began to wander as Valdes continued to talk. What had happened to the friendship we shared with the Timucua? Had our soldiers stole from the Indians too? Where was Lagundu? Did he now think of me as his enemy too? I listened once again to the sad defeated words of Pedro de Valdes.

"The Timucua demanded gifts every time they visited us. After while there was no more colorful cloth to give them."

"I will send for crossbows and padded jackets to help defend us against the Indians' swift arrows. If the French hear of our troubles here in Florida they are sure to return! We must stay strong! I will not accept defeat! We will empty half of the supply

66

ship here and leave one hundred men behind. Then we will sail to the fort – St. Matthew and pour out the other half and another one hundred men will remain there. I hope to stop the traitors' mutinous ships from sailing by offering them food *and amnesty!*" explained Menendez.

I now knew my captain was desperate. *So desperate*, that to save St. Augustine, he was willing to forgive his *mutinous* soldiers.

We sailed into the St. Johns River and found the two ships loading supplies from the fort at St. Matthew. Pedro Menendez kept his word and offered these traitors food and forgiveness. However, to Menendez's disappointment, few men surrendered and joined him. The two ships sailed away into an approaching storm. We did not pursue them. However, Menendez made sure after they departed that all the traitors' names were sent to New Spain. There, their fame would be the gallows and their fortunes only a dream!

Chapter VII- The Guale

It was springtime again and the air smelled of flowering trees as we sailed north from the fort at St. Matthew aboard the mother ship, the Santa Catalina, with two smaller convoy ships. The coastline appeared to have no mainland, only small and big islands. However, the sea was deep and we sailed easily north. The strong north winds of the winter were now a thing of the past.

"Our captain does not give up very easily, does he?" asked my friend Gomez as we busily assembled small Christian crosses made out of two sticks tied with string, which we had been instructed to do by Captain Menendez.

"No, he will not stop until he has explored every inch of Florida's coastline!" I said as I looked up at my hero, Pedro Menendez, while he examined the seaside from the bridge of our ship.

"Florida is very important to him," said old Ricardo as he walked over and examined one of our small crosses in his tanned rough hands.

"Yes," said Gomez nodding his head. Gomez was still not comfortable around old Ricardo with his one eye and many missing teeth. Old Ricardo was not easy to look at, I must admit.

"And his lost son is also important to him. Captain Menendez continues to seek him as well," I said as I tied two more sticks together.

It was three days later when we sailed into a harbor and

moored our ships. Old Ricardo, Gomez, and I along with fifty soldiers came ashore. Rosco and Diego were not allowed yet to set foot on land. They were being held in the brig of the Santa Catalina for mutiny. However, the two foolish sailors, Alonzo and Gonzalez, were permitted to join the exploration party.

"Be on guard men we might find some of the French survivors here," warned Menendez in a whisper as we rowed closer to the sandy shore of the inlet.

"WHAT DID HE SAY?" asked Alonzo in a loud voice.

"He said 'shut up, stupid!'" answered Gonzalez as he knocked Alonzo's hat off. Gonzalez was sitting behind Alonzo rowing the captain's boat.

As we rowed closer we could see a small dried-up cornfield and then palm-thatched houses.

"Look, Captain!" said old Ricardo as he pointed towards a group of forty Indians coming down a sandy path with their bows drawn.

Their arrows were pointed at us! They wore very little except for a feather on their heads and their bodies were smeared with red berry juice and black soot from their fires. They were a scary sight!

"THIS IS CRAZY! LET'S TURN AROUND!" exclaimed Alonzo and Gonzalez as they stopped rowing towards the shore.

"NO! We must not act scared! Raise your rifles men!" ordered Menendez to his soldiers.

I felt my hands begin to shake as I held on tightly to the oars. I had no rifle to raise. I looked at the hands of my friend, Gomez, and saw he too shook with fear. All at once, to our surprise, one of the Indians stepped forward and spoke in Spanish just as our boats drifted to shore.

"HELLO FRIENDS! DON'T SHOOT!" the Indian shouted.

I hoped in that moment that our captain had at last found his lost son, Juan. However, to my dismay, and I am sure to his also, the young man was another castaway. He introduced himself as "William" and explained that he had been left behind by the French to learn the Indians' language, but the French had never returned for him. He was to become their interpreter. However, William had not heard about the fate of the French men from Fort Caroline.

"You speak Spanish very well," said Pedro Menendez as he shook hands with William on the sandy beach. By this time, the Indians and soldiers had laid down their weapons as Menendez exited the craft.

"I was born in Spain, but later my family moved to France," answered William.

"What are these Indians' called?" asked Menendez pointing to the strange Indians standing behind William.

"They are the Guale tribe," answered William.

I couldn't help but notice how William was dressed just like a Guale Indian. He wore the red and black paint on his face, chest, arms, and legs along with seashells and pearl beads on his wrists and upper arms. It was hard to tell William apart from the Indians. He had learned more than just their language.

Menendez continued to speak, "I have brought food. Come, let's eat and talk. I have much to ask you, William. Rocco! Gomez! Bring the sea biscuits, figs, and honey!"

The Guale Indians laid down their bows and arrows and sat down on the sandy beach to eat with the soldiers. The Indians enjoyed our food. They seemed very hungry.

"William, are there any more French men here and what about any Spanish men?" asked my captain.

"No, just me," answered William as he bit into his hard sea biscuit.

"I see," said Menendez with disappointment in his voice. Then he next asked, "Tell me about the Guale Indians. Do they have a chief?"

"Yes. I will take you to him. I am sure he would like to meet you. The Guale Indians are now at war with the Ortista Indians that live to the north of here. Soon the Guale will sacrifice two Ortista Indians, which are their captives, to their rain god.

"Why?" asked the startled Menendez.

"Because it has not rained in eight months! See, their cornfields are dried up!" explained William pointing in the direction of the dry field.

"There is no such god as a rain god! Their rain god is nothing but a Devil! Take me to the Guale chief!" demanded Pedro Menendez.

With William as Menendez's interpreter, my captain not only convinced the Guale chief not to kill the two Ortista Indians but also to give them to him!

"I will leave some of my finest men here with you in exchange for these two Ortista men. I will return after I have made peace between the Guale and Ortista. While I am gone my men will teach you about my god," explained Menendez to the Guale Indian chief.

71

The Guale chief was *very, very* old, even older than old Ricardo. When our captain gave him an ax for a gift, his toothless grin was wide and wrinkled. The Guale chief's face looked just like the wrinkled fig that he tried to chew.

"I would like to know more about this god of yours," answered the old Guale chief.

"Good! Alonzo! Gonzalez! You two will stay behind and preach. We will now place a large cross in your village. Rocco! Gomez! Pass out your little crosses to all the Guale Indians!" ordered Pedro Menendez with a smile wider than the chiefs.

"Stay behind?" asked Alonzo with disbelief.

"You mean stay here with these Indians?" asked Gonzalez.

"Yes!" said Menendez as he turned and walked away.

"Gonzalez, do we have to dress like them?" asked Alonzo looking over at the Indians.

"Don't be stupid! Of course, we do! Just look at William!" answered the ignorant Gonzalez.

Chapter VIII- Santa Elena

We set sail once again, but this time with three new passengers – the two captive Ortista Indians whose lives Menendez had saved and William, the French castaway.

The Ortista Indians had never ridden on such a large ship before. The two of them swayed while trying to find their sea legs. They pored over every inch of the deck from afar with their eyes only. However, they were most amazed by the dwarf, Manuel, as he danced to Alfonso's fiddle.

"William, follow me to my quarters. I have a shirt, a pair of britches, and a hat for you," said Pedro Menendez as he led William, the French castaway, to his quarters.

"Menendez should clothe these two fool Indians also," said Diego, one of the two unkind soldiers that were now out of the brig. (Menendez again was desperate and needed all able hands on deck.)

"They wouldn't understand what to do with the clothes. They would probably try to put the britches on their arms and wear the shirt sleeves on their legs!" teased Rosco laughing.

Diego chuckled too. Gomez and I knew to hold our tongues.

The next day we came to the land of the Ortista Indians. It was a big harbor with a large white sandy island in the center. However, we saw no signs of the Ortista – no dried-up fields of corn or palm-thatched houses.

The two Ortista Indians pointed in the direction of a river that flowed into the harbor.

"Moor the ship! We will board the two smaller ships and sail up the river," commanded Menendez.

We continued on our way until we discovered the Ortista Indian village. The two Ortista Indians' faces changed from smiles to frowns as we approached their village. The village had been burned, no doubt by their enemy – the Guale! However, suddenly from the ashes came a group of survivors that were *not* glad to see us! Their arrows filled the air and landed in the river's dark water before us. The two Ortista Indians on board waved their arms and called out to them. The Ortista Indians on shore dropped their bows and rushed to the river's edge to greet their friends, the former Guale prisoners. They were also happy to see William. William, we discovered, was the husband of their chief's daughter!

Chapter IX- The Chief of Heaven

Pedro Menendez was successful! He helped the Ortista and Guale Indians become friends. The Ortista Indians also wanted to learn about our god after they found out the Guale were becoming Christian. Finally, the Ortista Indians agreed to allow Menendez to build a fort on the sandy island in the middle of their wide harbor.

I was very proud of my captain! We now weighed anchor and sailed south back to the Guale Indians to tell them the good news and pick up Alonzo and Gonzalez, who were there teaching the Guale Indians about our one god. When we reached the land of the Guale, Menendez went to the house of their chief.

"Welcome, Pedro Menendez. I am puzzled. Why has it not rained? The sun still burns brightly in the blue sky drying up our fields of corn. I have given Alonzo and Gonzalez many gifts for praying for rain for the Guale, but nothing has happened! I have made friends with the Ortista and spared two lives just as you asked of me. Why then does your Chief in Heaven not answer their prayers?"

William turned and spoke the chief's sorrowful words to Pedro Menendez who answered, "This is because *you* should have prayed to God – all the Guale Indians should have, *not* just Alonzo and Gonzalez. They have tricked you for presents! I will punish them!" exclaimed the angry Menendez looking now at the two foolish sailors dressed like the Guale Indians – smeared with the red and black paint.

"No! I will pray now to your Chief in Heaven," said the Guale chief as he walked outside the house and knelt at the large cross.

"I will pray with you," said Menendez as he joined the chief and also knelt at the cross.

I knelt too where I stood and so did all the others both Spanish and Guale men.

Suddenly, I felt a cool breeze upon my hot face. When I lifted my face to the sky I noticed grey clouds. Next came a flash of lightning and then a low rumble of thunder in the distance. A miracle of God! Rain now poured from the heavens. Our prayers had been answered once more!

Chapter X- The Search is Over

"SPAIN!" "FRIENDS!" "CHRISTIANS!" BROTHERS!" shouted Indians from their canoes as they paddled out to greet our ships along our voyage south to St. Matthew and St. Augustine. The news had spread about the rain and the Chief of Heaven – our God. Gomez and I threw the Indians the little wooden crosses as fast as we could make them. The Indians fought over the crosses as if they were made of gold. They truly believed the crosses were magical. It would take time for the Florida Indians to understand our Christian religion.

While Gomez and I worked long hours making the small crosses from two sticks tied together with string, the two foolish sailors, Alonzo and Gonzalez, swabbed the decks in our place for punishment.

When we arrived at St. Matthew our captain's spirits were good, however, his mood changed quickly. He was told that the Timucua Indians were now on the warpath. Their fire arrows had burned down the St. Augustine fort! We now made haste to St. Augustine where the people there needed not only shelter but food.

"We will build a new fort far away from the Timucua village. It will rest across the River of Dolphins on the island," said Pedro Menendez to Pedro de Valdes.

"Yes. We will work night and day until it is finished!" exclaimed Pedro de Valdes.

"It would be wiser to work when the sun is not so hot," advised Menendez.

"Good idea! We will work at night and early in the day!" said the eager Pedro de Valdes.

Everyone worked long hours building the new fort and ferrying what goods were left at the old fort to the new site. On one such trip to the old fort, I heard my name called from afar - "Rocco….Rocco" It was not the voice of my friend, Gomez. He was back on the island building the new fort. However, the voice sounded familiar. I turned around and saw a young Timucua man hiding behind a tree – it was Lagundu!

"Lagundu!" I whispered as I carefully rushed over to greet my Indian friend behind the big tree draped with moss. We both stayed hidden for we knew it was not safe for him here.

Lagundu pointed to himself first and said, "Lagundu is Rocco's friend!" He next pointed to me and asked, "Rocco, Lagundu, friend?"

"Yes," I said smiling. It was good to see Lagundu again. I thought I never would see him again. He still wore my shirt, although, he could no longer button it and Gomez's old boots with the holes in the toes. Lagundu's toes stuck out even further now. And, I still wore his necklace made of tiny bones, seashells, and fish teeth.

"Lagundu, sorry," he said as he pointed to the burned fort.

The Timucua had been our friends. I wondered what had gone wrong. "Rocco, sorry too," I said as I thought to myself how sad it was that Lagundu and I could no longer be friends like we once were when we first met.

"Good-bye, Rocco," said Lagundu as he vanished from my sight for the last time.

"Good-bye, Lagundu."

Pedro Menendez, the Adelantado of Florida, had tried his

best to carry out King Philip of Spain's contract for Florida – to map the coastline, to build forts that would protect Spain's treasure ships, and lastly to persuade the Indians to be our friends and become Christian. Of course, my captain also had his own agenda – to find his lost son, Juan. Sadly, he had not been successful in all his quests. Menendez's time in Florida was now coming to an end.

"My search is over. I have to return to Spain and tell Juan's mother her boy is gone from this life," said Menendez to Pedro de Valdes. "I have no more money. But I will travel to Cuba and speak to Governor Osorio once more. Somehow I will find food and supplies for Florida!"

"It seems King Philip has forgotten about us. We will pray for you, Pedro Menendez, and for St. Augustine," said Pedro de Valdes as Menendez boarded his ship for Havana, Cuba once again.

I could see the despair in both men's eyes and I too for the first time worried about Spanish Florida's future.

As we headed out to sea once more, our hopes were low, but we, like our captain, were not ready to give up. We had come so far and still had much to do. I climbed up into the crow's nest and closed my eyes, clasped my hands tightly, and knelt my head before saying a prayer. When I opened my eyes there sailing on the horizon was one of King Philip's Spanish ships loaded with supplies and food heading in Florida's direction! My prayers had been answered once again! King Philip had not forgotten us! St. Augustine would survive!

The End

Part III- Historical Summary

Pedro Menendez headed south on foot with his men after leaving St. Augustine. Two supply ships followed them along the coast. Their first native encounter was with the Ais (Eye-ees) Indians that lived along the Indian River near present-day Vero Beach. These Indians had a bad reputation. For over twenty years they had taken advantage of Spanish shipwrecks – killing the survivors and collecting the booty for themselves. They dressed in buckskin and dyed red cloth. They wore carved shell necklaces and gorget-shaped pendants and Spanish gold and silver jewelry. Their homes were similar to the Timucua with benches that lined the interior walls for resting. Palmetto mats were used on the benches as well as for curtains and they used pillows stuffed with Spanish moss.

Pedro Menendez made a treaty with the Ais Indians. The Indians promised peace, obedience, and loyalty to the King of Spain – Philip II. Menendez sealed the treaty with the offering of clothing and an ax for the chief. Menendez left some of his men at the Jupiter Inlet to build Ft. Santa Lucia. Only a few of these men would survive and escape the Indian's attacks and starvation by seizing a relief ship – the Ascension.

Pedro Menendez next headed for Cuba in two small ships (pataches). When Menendez reached Havana, Cuba he was pleased to discover that three of the original ships left behind during the crossing from Spain had arrived. The two ships were supposed to have met Menendez for the crossing but had not shown up in time. Menendez sent one ship for Florida with its cargo and the other ship to the search for more goods for Florida in the Caribbean. These Spanish ships had also captured a Portuguese ship which

Menendez auctioned off for food and goods for the Florida settlements.

The royal governor of Cuba, Garcia Osorio, never would cooperate with Pedro Menendez. Menendez represented a threat of power to Osorio. Osorio probably feared that Menendez wanted his position as the royal governor of Cuba. While in Cuba, Menendez arranged the possession of a Spanish flagship named the Santa Catalina for his Florida exploration. He left Cuba with seven ships and 500 men.

Pedro Menendez sailed around the Florida Keys and up the western coast of Florida. A Spanish castaway named Hernando Escalante Fontaneda was discovered near Charlotte Harbor – Ft. Meyers area. There were four to seven thousand Calusa Indians in this area and Hernando was one of fourteen of their captives. Originally there were forty-two captives; however, many had been sacrificed as was a custom of the Calusa.

The chief of the Calusa Indians was Chief Carlos, a nice looking man in his twenties. Another custom of the Calusa Indians was to marry siblings. Chief Carlos was not only married to his pretty young wife, but also to his unattractive thirty-five-year-old sister whom he gave as a present to Pedro Menendez as his wife. Menendez tried to explain to Chief Carlos that he was already married and that he couldn't marry a non-Christian, but Chief Carlos said that they were now all Christians since he had adopted Menendez as his brother.

Pedro Menendez gave Chief Carlos' sister a Christian name (Antonia) and baptized her before marrying her. Menendez took Antonia and several captives back to Cuba. Later he would return the homesick Antonia to her brother Chief Carlos.

When Pedro Menendez returned to St. Augustine he

discovered a mutiny had begun a couple of months earlier in both forts - St. Matthew and St. Augustine. The winter had been long and cold and there was little loot or entertainment for the men. The hard water had made the people of St. Augustine sick with fever. Their stomachs had swelled and many had lost their appetites. The Timucua Indians had become their enemies and the soldiers' weapons once discharged could not be reloaded quickly enough before four or five arrows were fired at him. A total of one hundred people had lost their lives.

A supply ship, the Conception, loaded with food and supplies for St. Augustine had been seized by 120 men there. And an unfinished French ship was completed at St. Matthew (the former French Fort Caroline) and one hundred men there sailed with the Conception for the Caribbean in a storm. Pedro Menendez made sure their mutinous names preceded them to their destinations. Menendez also ordered padded jackets for his soldiers and cross-bows to fight the Timucua Indians.

Pedro Menendez sailed north of St. Augustine and St. Matthew to continue the exploration of Florida's coastline in the spring of 1566. His first landing was at St. Catherine's Island where he discovered the Guale (Gwal-lee) Indians and also a Frenchman named William Rufin or in another account he was named Matthew Guillermo. This Frenchman had been left by Ribault's 1562 expedition to become an interpreter. Menendez exchanged six of his men, including one of his nephews, for two Ortista Indians being held by the Guale, their enemy. His goal was to bring peace to the area.

Pedro Menendez found the Ortista Indians at a harbor named by the French as Port Royal. It was six miles across and approximately 150 miles north of St Matthew (Jacksonville, Fl.).

Today this area is called Hilton Head, South Carolina. Menendez built a fort there on the island known as Parris Island, South Carolina. He also named this area Santa Elena and the capital of Florida. One hundred and ten men were assigned to the fort before Menendez left after a treaty between the Indians. Pedro Menendez was adopted by both Indian chiefs as their brothers. He gave both a gift of an ax. (It was not the custom of the Spanish to give the Indians firearms.)

Pedro Menendez left Florida for Spain on May 18, 1567. He left with thirty-two men including Pedro de Valdes (his daughter's fiancé), his son-in-law Hernando Mirando, and other family members and close friends. Menendez arrived in his hometown of Avilles in July 1567 and visited his wife and daughters after a twenty-year absence! He had only been home four times in eighteen years while in King Philip's service. Pedro Menendez returned briefly to Florida in 1571.

While in Spain, Menendez tried to persuade young married men and their families to settle in Florida, by offering them free land. This was Spanish Florida's weakness – its inability to attract enough settlers. It remained mostly a military outpost for the other Spanish colonies in Mexico, Central America, and the Caribbean Islands. Although, Pedro Menendez did whatever it took to settle Florida - He set up a pipeline of supplies that he had to purchase with his own over-extended funds, sold his own goods, begged, borrowed, bartered, hunted corsairs, and even put men to death!

Pedro Menendez died of typhoid fever at the age of 55 years old on September 17, 1574. He had recently been named by King Philip the Captain-General of the Spanish Armada. It was the largest armada ever with 150 ships and 12,000 troops. Menendez died ten days later at the armada harbor of Santander, Spain. Nine days before his death he wrote his nephew in St. Augustine, Pedro

Menendez Marquez (the ninth anniversary of St. Augustine) - "After the salvation of my soul, there is nothing in this world that I desire more than to see myself in Florida."

Menendez was buried in a plain brown robe bound by a cord and drawn over his head. Menendez was a 3rd order Franciscan. On August 6, 1924, Menendez's body was placed in a new mausoleum in a new lead coffin and richly carved sarcophagus in Aviles. The gift of the original coffin and was presented to a delegation from St. Augustine in 1926 and brought back to St. Augustine. Sadly it was not displayed in a place of honor for many years but rather found in an unused room of the St. Augustine City Hall. It was surrounded by litter and was literally forgotten by the town he founded. Today it is displayed at Nombre de Dios Mission of St. Augustine in its small museum close to the site where he landed.

There is a statue of Pedro Menendez in front of the Lightner Museum, formerly the Alcazar Hotel at 75 King Street. The statue is the replica of the original found in Menendez's home of Aviles, Spain.

Who's Who?- Character Reference Guide

(Alphabetical order)

1. <u>Alfonso</u> – (Al-fond-so) fictional name for Spanish musician on board Menendez's ship

2. <u>Alonzo</u> – (Ah-lawn-so) fictional Spanish sailor on board Menendez's ship

3. <u>Antonia</u> – (And-tone-knee-ah) Calusa Indian princess that married Pedro Menendez

4. <u>Carlos</u> – (Car-lows) Chief of the Calusa Indians

5. <u>Diego</u> – (Dee-a-go) fictional Spanish soldier on board Menendez's ship

6. <u>Gomez</u> – (Go-mezz) fictional Spanish cabin boy on board Menendez' ship

7. <u>Gonzalez</u> – (Gun-zall-ezz) fictional Spanish sailor on board Menendez's ship

8. <u>Hernando</u> – (Her-nan-doe) Spanish castaway living with the Calusa Indians

9. <u>Indians Native to Florida</u> – <u>Ais</u> (Eye-ease), <u>Calusa</u> (Caw-loo-sah), <u>Guale</u> (Gwal-lee), <u>Ortista</u> (Or-tease-tah), <u>Timucua</u> (Tee-moo-quah)

10. <u>Lagundu</u> – (La-goon-do) fictional Timucua Indian boy; Native American name meaning "Peace"

11. <u>Rene' de Laudonniere</u> (Ruh- nay day low-don-yair) – Frenchman responsible for the construction of Ft. Caroline on the St. John's River (the River May)

12. <u>Manuel</u> – (Man-you-el) fictional name for the little person/clown that entertained Menendez on his ship

13. <u>Juan Menendez</u> – (Wand Main-ain-days) Pedro Menendez's missing son

14. <u>Pedro Menendez de Aviles y Alonso de la Campa</u> – (Pay-throw Main-ain-days) Feb. 15, 1519 – Sept. 17, 1574, Spanish naval officer and founder and colonizer of the nation's oldest existing city – St. Augustine, Florida.

15. <u>Garcia Osorio</u> – (Gar-see-ah Oh-sore-e-oh) Spanish governor of Cuba

16. <u>Philip II</u> – King of Spain from 1565 – 1598

17. <u>Jean Ribault</u> – (Ree-bow) Frenchman defeated by Menendez at Matanzas Inlet

18. <u>Ricardo</u> – (Ree-car-doe) fictional old Spanish sailor on board Menendez's ship

19. <u>Rocco</u> – (Rock-coe) fictional Spanish cabin boy on board Menendez's ship and main character telling the story

20. <u>Rosco</u> – (Raw-skoe) fictional Spanish soldier on board Menendez's ship

21. <u>Chief Seloy</u> – (Say-low-ee) Timucua Indian chief at St. Augustine

22. <u>Pedro de Valdes</u> – (Val-dees) Pedro Menendez's son-in-law and officer on board Menendez's ship and in charge at St. Augustine

23. <u>William</u> – French youth discovered living with the Guale and Ortista Indians

Timeline- When Did It Happen?

February 15, 1519   Birth of Pedro Menendez de Aviles y Alonso De la Campa at Aviles in Asturias (Spain)

1533   Pedro Menendez runs away from home to become a sailor

1549   King of Spain commissions Menendez to fight pirates off the coastline of Spain

1559   Menendez is General of the Armada of the Spanish Crown

1561   Menendez commands the largest treasure fleet from Mexico to Spain – one of the vessels containing his son disappears

1563 – 1565   Menendez is jailed for twenty months by the House of Trade

May 22, 1565   Ribault sails for Florida

June 29, 1565   Menendez sails for Florida

September 8, 1565 Menendez lands in St. Augustine (42 years before Jamestown and 55 years before the Pilgrims landed at Plymouth Rock)

September 20, 1565 Menendez attacks Ft. Caroline

September 29, 1565 Death of French castaways at Matanzas

October 10, 1565   Death of Ribault at Matanzas Inlet

Winter of 1565-'66 Menendez explores Florida's coast – meets Indians – Ais and

Calusa – married Antonia

Spring of 1566   Mutiny at Ft. Santa Lucia and Treason at St. Augustine –

Menendez met and made peace between Guale and Ortista Indian
            tribes of Georgia and South Carolina (Hilton Head)

1567   Menendez returns to Spain

1571   Menendez returns to Florida for a brief stay

September 17, 1574   The death of Pedro Menendez while in Spain

Nautical Terminology- What Was That?

1. astrolabe – an early compass

2. below – under the main deck

3. booty – rewards of treasure

4. bow – front part of a ship

5. bridge – elevated platform above the main deck where the ship is navigated

6. brig – a ship's jail

7. crow's nest – a small platform high up on a mast where a crew member keeps a lookout

8. fathom – measure of depth (1 fathom equals 6 feet)

9. forecastle – raised deck in front of the foremast where cannons may be mounted

10. foremast – the mast found in the front (bow) of a ship

11. galley – ship's kitchen

12. hatch – the opening in the deck where cargo is loaded in the hold

13. helm – a ship's steering wheel

14. hold – area below deck where cargo is stored

15. hull – body of a sailboat/ship

16. knot – one nautical mile per hour

17. league – measure of distance (1 league equals about 3 miles)

18. marlin spikes - railing

19. mast – long vertical pole on the deck of a ship used to hold the sails

20. middle gun deck – found under main deck with cannons lined on either side pointed through port holes with a low cramped ceiling

21. moor – to anchor ship

22. nautical mile – distance used for sea navigation (1 nautical mile equals 6076.115 feet)

23. poop – a short raised deck at the rear of a ship

24. port side – left side of a ship when facing the brow

25. port hole – a window on the side of a ship

26. prow – front of a ship

27. quarterdeck – ran from the mainmast to the rear of the ship where a still still higher deck called the poop was located.

28. rigging – the lines (ropes) used on a ship to work the sails

29. rudder – attached to the stern under water to cause the ship to turn

30. sailing across the wind – will cause the fastest speed the sailing ship can sail

31. sailing before the wind – will cause a slower speed for a sailing ship

32. sailing into the wind – tacking

33. starboard side – the right side of a ship

34. stern – the rear part of a ship

35. swab the deck – wash the deck

36. tacking – to change the direction of a sailing ship

37. ton – equals 2,000 pounds

38. weigh anchor – to pull the anchor of the ship up from the bottom

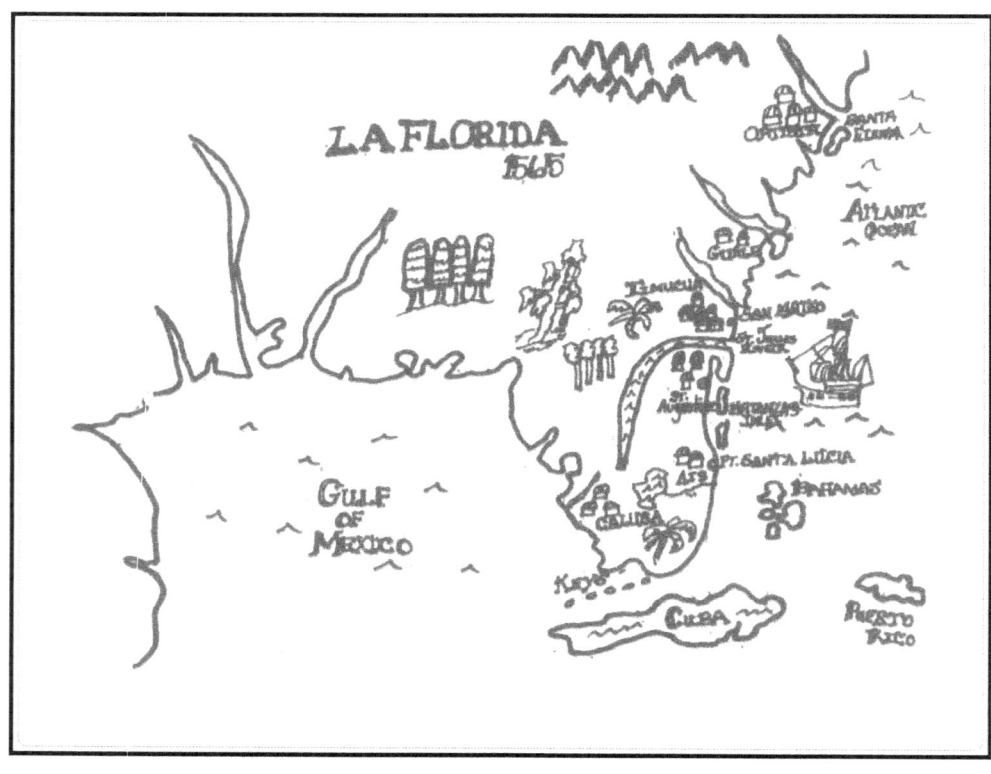

Bibliography- How Do You Know That?

A Foothold in Florida, by Sarah Lawson, Antique Atlas Publications, West Sussex, England, Castle Cary Press, Sumerset, England, Aug. 1992.

Don Pedro Menendez de Avilles, Captain General of the Ocean Sea Under King Felipe II of Spain, by Justo Urena Y Hevia, translated March 21, 2000

Florida's First People by Robin C. Brown, Pineapple Press, Inc., Sarasota, Fl., copyright 1994.

Menendez: Pedro Menendez de Aviles – Captain General of the Ocean Sea by Albert Manucy, Pineapple Press, Inc. Sarasota, Fl., copyright 1983, published 1992

Miami Herald Newspaper – "Tales of Old Florida Buried in Spain" by Joe Crankshaw, 11/3/97.

National Geographic Vol. 173 No. 3 – "Exploring our Forgotten Century" pp. 330-362, March 1988.

Pedro Menendez de Aviles' by Gonzalo Solis de Meras', translated by Jeanette Thurber Connor, University Press, Gainesville, Fl., 1964.

Pedro Menendez de Aviles' – Founder of Florida by Bartolome Barrvientos, translated by Anthony Kerrigan, University Press, Gainesville, Fl., 1965.

St. Augustine Historical Society – 271 Charlotte St., Research Library, Aviles St., St. Augustine, Fl., librarian Charles Tingley, researcher – Leslie Wilson.

The Enterprise of Florida: Pedro Menendez de Aviles' and Spanish

Conquest of 1565 – 1568, by Eugene Lyon, University Press of Florida, Gainesville, Fl., Copyright 1974 & 1976.

The New World: The First Pictures of America by John White and Jacques Le Moyne and engraved by Theodore De Bry, Edited and annotated by Stefan Lorant Duell, Sloan, & Pearce, New York

The Sea Tiger – The Story of Pedro Menendez by Frank Kolars, Hawthorne Book, New York, copyright 1963

The St. Augustine Evening Record Newspaper Vol. XLIII, No. 193, Oct. 9, 1924, "Delegation Returns from Spain"

The St. Augustine Record Newspaper, "Menendez the Navigator" by Jason Scott – Compass Editor, pp. 8 & 9, Oct. 1, 1997.

The St. Augustine Record Newspaper, "Find Out More About the Founder Of St. Augusine" by Natalie & Tommy Lucas, Sept. 1, 1998.

U.S. Dept. of the Interior, National Park Service, S.E. Nat'l Monuments –   Office of the Coordinating Superintendent of St.Augustine, Fl., "Great Men and Great Events in The History of St. Augusine, Florida," Pedro Menendez de Avilles Radio Program – WFOY St. Augustine, Fl., February 9, 1939, 7:30, Thurs.

World Book Encyclopedia, Vol. 17, p. 409 & p. 416, by World Book Inc.,   Chicago, Ill., copyright 1988.

www.adp.fsu.edu/fleet.html

www.ancientnative.org

www.bartleby.com

www.corpun.com

www.enchantedlearning.com

www.floridahistory.org

http://floridaindiansmounds.com

www.hartford-hwp.com

www.infoplease.com

www.jacksonvillestory.com

www.kings.edu/womens_history/cathymedici.html

www.publicbookshelf.com

www.rootsweb.com

www.staugustine.com

www.wikipedia.org

ABOUT THE AUTHOR

L. L. Eadie is passionate about writing and reading - especially for young adults. Before she was published her works earned her Florida Writers' Association's Royal Palm Literary Awards. She credits her success not only for being an active member of both FWA and the Society of Children's Book Writers and Illustrators, but also belonging to several critique groups over the past ten plus years she's been writing.

She is a proud Gator graduate of the University of Florida - holding a Bachelor of Arts degree in Education. She taught numerous years, grades, subjects, and children.

She is inspired daily and often nightly when her muse wakes her with a fabulous new idea or pressing story to be written.

To get in contact with the author check out her website and

social media pages.

Facebook Page: https://www.facebook.com/L-L-Eadie-141069182765272/

Twitter Account: https://twitter.com/lindaeadie

Amazon Profile Page: https://www.amazon.com/-/e/B084M7TK7T

Website: https://lindaeadie.wixsite.com/booksbylleadie/

YouTube Channel: https://www.youtube.com/channel/UCOqwdnT40rPwg7HSE6GmKlg

Email: LLEadieauthor@gmail.com

www.ingramcontent.com/pod-product-compliance
Lightning Source LLC
Chambersburg PA
CBHW060943120626
46557CB00003B/1120